·OLIVER·
TWIST

by Charles Dickens

Retold by Brenda Ralph Lewis and Ronne Randall
Illustrated by John Holder

'Please, sir… I want some more'

OLIVER'S EARLY LIFE

In a workhouse some eighty miles from London, a baby boy was born one evening. His mother, a beautiful young woman, had been found lying in the street the night before. No one knew who she was or where she was from, and she died within minutes of giving birth. Mr Bumble, the man in charge of the workhouse, named the baby Oliver Twist.

Until he was nine, Oliver lived with a woman who looked after orphans for a small fee. Then Mr Bumble took him back to the workhouse, to learn a trade with other boys his age.

Oliver was miserable at the workhouse, and he was always hungry. The boys were fed nothing but gruel. One evening, after finishing his portion of gruel, Oliver thought he would go mad with hunger. Holding out his bowl, he approached the master of the workhouse.

'Please, sir,' said Oliver, 'I want some more.'

The master was stupefied. No one had *ever* dared to ask for more! Enraged, he struck Oliver on the head and locked him up in a dismal cell, where he remained for weeks.

Oliver was rescued by Mr Sowerberry, an undertaker who took him on as an apprentice. But when Oliver got into a fight with Mr Sowerberry's assistant, the undertaker threatened to send him back to the workhouse.

The thought was unbearable to Oliver. In desperation, he decided to run away.

Oliver sat on a doorstep

OLIVER COMES TO LONDON

Oliver sat on a doorstep and shivered. The sun was just rising, and he was too exhausted to move. He had walked seventy miles since running away from Mr Sowerberry. His feet were sore and bleeding, he ached all over, and he was weak with hunger. But even this was better than the workhouse.

Some time later, Oliver saw a rough-looking boy standing close by, looking him up and down with sharp little eyes.

'Hello!' said the boy chirpily. 'What are you doing here?'

'I'm hungry and tired,' Oliver replied weakly. 'I'm trying to get to London, and I've been walking for seven days.'

The boy whistled in wonderment. Then he gave Oliver a kind look. 'You'll be wanting grub. Don't worry, I'll pay!'

When Oliver had wolfed down the first real meal he had had for days, the boy asked: 'Got any lodgings in London?'

'No,' said Oliver ruefully.

'I know a nice old gent in London who'll give you a bed for nothing,' said the boy. He sounded very confident.

This offer of a place to sleep, and a free place at that, was extremely tempting, and Oliver accepted gratefully.

'What's your name?' asked the boy. When Oliver told him, he said, 'I'm Jack Dawkins – they call me the Artful Dodger!'

Oliver was none too sure that someone with a name like that was an honest person, but he was so grateful for the Dodger's help that he said nothing.

— ✳ —

FAGIN'S GANG

Oliver did not know yet that the Dodger belonged to a gang of pickpockets and thieves. The Dodger's 'old gent', whose name was Fagin, was their ringleader.

'Come in, my boy!' Fagin welcomed Oliver. He was a shrivelled-up, villainous-looking creature, but he gave Oliver a meal and showed him an old mattress where he could sleep.

In the days that followed, the Dodger and the other boys brought home things that Oliver was told to sort out. He never suspected that these things were stolen until one day when he went out with the Dodger and a boy called Charley Bates.

The boys seemed to wander aimlessly until the Dodger suddenly halted in a passageway. 'He'll do for us,' he whispered, pointing to a well-dressed gentleman by a bookstall.

Charley and the Dodger slipped across to where the man was standing. As Oliver watched in alarm, the Dodger plunged his hand into the man's pocket, drew out a handkerchief and handed it to Charley. Then they both fled.

Oliver felt a tingle of terror. It was out and out stealing, and he was involved! He began to run away, but it was too late. The old gentleman, whose name was Mr Brownlow, had discovered that his silk handkerchief was missing.

'Stop, thief!' he cried, setting off after Oliver. A crowd of people joined him, and a big man soon overtook Oliver. One blow from the man's fist sent Oliver sprawling into the mud.

Fagin was a… villainous-looking creature

'Who are you?' Mr Fang demanded crossly

NEW FRIENDS

Someone called a policeman; Oliver was bundled off to the nearest police station, and Mr Brownlow followed. Curiously, he seemed to regret the whole business, and said so when Oliver was taken before the magistrate, Mr Fang.

'This boy is not a thief, sir. I am sure of it!' Mr Brownlow protested. 'Please deal kindly with him. Besides, I believe he is ill.'

Oliver did indeed look very unwell. All of a sudden, he fell to the floor in a faint.

Just then, an elderly man came rushing into the courtroom. 'Stop! Stop!' he cried.

'Who are you?' Mr Fang demanded crossly.

'I keep the bookstall in the passageway!' the newcomer explained. 'The robbery was committed by another boy, not this poor young fellow!' He pointed to Oliver, still unconscious on the floor.

Mr Fang frowned, and started grumbling about people wasting his time. He could do nothing except dismiss the charge against Oliver.

Oliver was thrown onto the pavement outside the courtroom, where he was soon found by Mr Brownlow.

'Dear me, how pale he is! And he's shivering! He has a fever, I'll be bound!' Mr Brownlow bent down beside Oliver, regarding him anxiously. 'Call a coach, somebody, directly!'

The next thing Oliver knew was that he was in bed in a quiet, shady room. 'What place is this?' he murmured.

A plump, motherly looking old lady appeared beside the bed. There was a sweet, loving expression on her face.

'Hush, dear!' she said softly. 'You must stay quiet now, or you will be ill again!'

The lady's name was Mrs Bedwin, and she was Mr Brownlow's housekeeper. For several more days, she looked after Oliver and saw to his every need, until at last he was well enough to be visited by Mr Brownlow.

'And how do you feel now, dear boy?' the old gentleman wanted to know.

'Oh, much better, sir, and very happy – very grateful indeed for all your goodness to me!'

As Oliver spoke, Mr Brownlow kept staring at him. This poor, neglected waif reminded him of someone, but whom? Then the answer came to him. Of course – the portrait! Mr Brownlow looked up at the picture hanging on the wall just above Oliver's head. It showed a pretty young lady. Mr Brownlow glanced at Oliver and gave a start.

'Mrs Bedwin!' he gasped. 'Don't you see? This boy – his eyes, his mouth, his expression – his whole face is the same as the face in the picture!'

'HE MUST BE FOUND'

Meanwhile, the Artful Dodger and Charley were in big trouble with Fagin for 'losing' Oliver in the street.

When they returned without him, Fagin flew into a rage and threatened to throttle both of them. Oliver now knew quite a lot about the gang and how they worked, so Fagin was worried in case the boy had 'peached' – that is, betrayed the gang to the police.

'He must be found, he must!' Fagin stormed.

'But – but how?' Charley Bates stuttered. 'London's an enormous place, Fagin. Where do we start?'

Fagin's fury suddenly faded away. A cunning gleam came into his eyes. 'Leave that to me, my boy,' he told Charley as he paced the room. 'I'll think of something!'

Fagin did not take long to come up with a plan. One of the thieves in the gang was a girl called Nancy. Fagin told her to go to the police station to see what she could find out about where Oliver was.

At first Nancy refused, for she was afraid of the police. She was more afraid, though, of Bill Sikes, another member of Fagin's gang and a cruel bully of a man.

'Say no, would you?' Bill glowered at Nancy, raising his hand. 'You'll get my fist in your face!' he threatened. It would not have been the first time Bill had beaten Nancy. 'All right, all right,' she said hastily. 'I'll go!'

— ✳ —

Fagin flew into a rage

If she had to run this errand, Nancy thought, she might as well make a good job of it. Nancy was a good actress, and when she got to the police station she burst into tears. Through her wails and sobs, she told the policeman that she had lost her dear little brother. She was lying and meant Oliver, of course.

'Where is he, oh, where is he?' Nancy wept. 'I must find him, I must!'

The policeman was a soft-hearted man, and he was totally deceived by Nancy's pretence. So he told her that the boy had been taken away by an old gentleman who lived somewhere near Pentonville in north London.

When Nancy returned with this news, Fagin immediately sent her out again, together with the Artful Dodger and Charley Bates, to search for the house in Pentonville.

'Oliver has not betrayed us yet!' Fagin muttered nervously. 'Nancy would've learned at the station had he done that! But he must be found before he can talk, or we are all lost!'

— ✳ —

TRAPPED

Oliver was going to fall into Fagin's hands much more easily than anyone thought. As he slowly recovered his health, he tried to think of some way to repay all the loving care he had received in Mr Brownlow's house. His chance came one day when a messenger delivered a parcel of books for Mr Brownlow, but left before he could be given some other volumes which Mr Brownlow had wanted to return to the shop.

'Please let me take them, sir!' Oliver begged. 'I won't be ten minutes! I'll run all the way!'

Oliver's eyes sparkled with eagerness as Mr Brownlow gave him the books and a five-pound note to cover the bill at the bookshop. Oliver set off briskly. He felt very smart in the new set of clothes Mr Brownlow had bought for him. They were the first new clothes Oliver had ever worn, for in the workhouse he wore only ragged old clothes other people had discarded.

He had nearly reached the bookshop when all of a sudden a young woman stepped into his path. She flung her arms round his neck, and to his amazement she started crying: 'Oh, my gracious! I've found him! My dear, lost little brother! I've found him!'

It was Nancy. She had just come out of a public house, where Fagin and Bill Sikes had been drinking and talking

Bill hit Oliver

together. She was holding Oliver very tightly as he struggled hard, trying to escape. 'You're not my sister! You're not! I haven't got a sister!' Oliver kept yelling.

Just then, he felt Mr Brownlow's books being snatched from him, and a heavy blow landed on the back of his head. Bill Sikes, hearing the noise and shouting, had come out of the public house to see Oliver struggling with Nancy. Bill hit Oliver again, then grabbed his collar and began dragging the dazed boy through a maze of narrow, winding streets to the place that Oliver dreaded even more than the terrible workhouse – Fagin's den.

'Delighted to see you looking so well, my boy!' Fagin said in a menacing voice that made Oliver shiver right down his spine. He was trapped! Oliver's heart sank when he thought of his new, kind friends at Mr Brownlow's house. What would they think when he did not return? Perhaps they would think he had run away with Mr Brownlow's five pounds and the valuable books, to say nothing of his fine, new suit of clothes.

'If they thought that, I could not bear it!' Oliver said to himself, feeling distraught.

THREATENING WORDS

During the next few days, Fagin made certain that Oliver had no chance to escape.

All the while, Mr Brownlow was frantically searching for Oliver. He sent out servants to scour the streets for the boy, and asked everyone he met if they had spotted him. He even put an advertisement in the newspaper, offering a reward for information about Oliver. But all his efforts achieved nothing. As far as Mr Brownlow knew, the boy had vanished.

In the meantime, Fagin was trying to train Oliver to be a criminal. He told him how exciting it was to go out thieving, and what a fortune he could make. Oliver did not believe him.

One day, Fagin told Oliver, 'I'm sending you over to Bill Sikes, my boy! We've a nice little job for you!'

Nancy came to collect Oliver. She seemed very upset.

Despite her rough ways and sharp tongue, Nancy had a kind heart. She had become very fond of Oliver, and she knew that he was in great danger now. Fagin and Bill Sikes planned to use him to help them in a big robbery.

At Bill's house, Bill took Oliver to one side. 'Do you know what this is?' he asked, showing Oliver a small pistol.

Oliver gulped and nodded. Bill loaded the pistol, then placed the barrel against Oliver's head. It felt cold and hard.

'We're going out, you and me,' Sikes growled. 'And if you speak a word to anyone, I'll blow your head off!'

— ✳ —

They all set off into the… night

THE BURGLARY

Bill Sikes took Oliver to a dank, dilapidated house well outside London. There, Sikes's two accomplices were waiting. After gathering up their pistols, crowbars and other equipment, they all set off into the pitch-black, foggy night.

Oliver now realised the frightful crime in which he was involved, and begged Bill Sikes to let him go. 'I'll never come near London again, I promise!' Oliver cried.

But Bill had a job for Oliver, and he meant to make sure he did it. When they reached the house where the robbery was to take place, Bill forced open a tiny window. 'Get in there!' he ordered Oliver. 'Then open the front door and let us in. And don't try any tricks, or I'll shoot you dead!'

Despite this threat, Oliver decided to try and warn the people in the house. Once inside, he started running upstairs to the family's rooms. 'Come back, you wretch!' cried Bill.

All at once, two men appeared at the top of the stairs. One held a lantern, the other a pistol. Oliver heard him fire it, and felt a sharp pain in his arm. There was a crash, another shot and the sound of a bell. Oliver felt himself being dragged outside.

The burglary had gone wrong. The two men in the house had raised the alarm, and Bill Sikes and his gang could only run, taking Oliver, too.

Oliver, dazed, barely knew what was going on. His arm hurt dreadfully. Blackness closed in on him, and he fainted.

— ✳ —

KINDNESS – AND
A DISAPPOINTMENT

When Oliver awoke, it was morning, and he was lying in a ditch, where Bill Sikes had left him. Bill and the other robbers were nowhere to be seen, for they had all managed to escape and had hurried back to London.

Oliver felt weak, and the shawl Bill had tied round his arm was soaked with blood. With a tremendous effort, he struggled to his feet and staggered along until he reached a road. A short way on, he came to a house. With a flicker of fear, he realised that it was the very house where the robbery had been attempted the previous night.

Oliver wanted to run away, but his strength failed him.

Inside, the servants heard a noise. When they opened the front door, one of them, Mr Giles, recognised Oliver.

'Here's the thief! I shot him!' he shouted.

'Giles!' a soft voice whispered from the top of the stairs. 'Hush, or you'll frighten my aunt!'

It was a young girl, very slender and sweet-faced, with kind, deep blue eyes. She came quietly down the stairs and looked at Oliver, who had been carried inside and was lying on the hall floor.

'Oh, the poor little fellow!' the girl exclaimed. 'Carry him upstairs, Giles. Gently now, be careful!'

The young lady, whose name was Rose, ordered the doctor to be brought. The bullet, the doctor discovered, had

— ✳ —

'Gently now, be careful!'

broken Oliver's arm. The injury was not serious, but it would be a long time before the arm mended and Oliver felt well again.

Rose, her aunt Mrs Maylie, the doctor, whose name was Losberne, and all the servants – even Giles – were very kind and gentle towards Oliver.

Oliver was very grateful for his good fortune, but all the same, he wanted more than anything to return to London and find Mr Brownlow.

Dr Losberne offered to take Oliver to London in his carriage. When they reached the street where Mr Brownlow lived, Oliver spotted the house at once. 'That one! There! The white house!' he cried, pointing excitedly.

But Oliver's excitement soon faded, for the house was all shut up and there was a notice outside saying 'To Let'. Dr Losberne sent his coachman next door to make enquiries, and he returned with the sad news that Mr Brownlow had gone away six weeks previously, far across the Atlantic Ocean to the West Indies.

Oliver burst into tears. It was all too terrible! Mr Brownlow must have left thinking Oliver was a deceitful, dishonest little wretch. Now he would never learn the truth.

A CURIOUS TALE

Dr Losberne took Oliver back to his friends in the country, and for a long time the boy was very sad. Oliver could not believe there would be a happy ending to his search – but there was.

Three months later, Dr Losberne took Oliver to London again, and Rose Maylie came with them. They were all delighted to discover that Mr Brownlow had returned and was very anxious for news of Oliver. The old gentleman greeted Oliver warmly and Mrs Bedwin, the housekeeper, hugged him and kissed him joyfully.

When all the greetings were over, and Oliver was well occupied telling Mrs Bedwin of his adventures, Rose asked Mr Brownlow if she could see him alone, for she had a secret to confide.

Mr Brownlow took Rose to a quiet room, where she told him a very curious tale.

A day or two before, a wretched young girl called Nancy had come to see Rose at her hotel in London. Nancy told Rose about a man called Monks, who had come to Fagin's house a few days earlier, while Nancy was there.

Fagin and Monks knew each other already, for they had planned the burglary at the house where Rose lived with Mrs Maylie. Fagin took Monks off to another room and Nancy, listening at the door, overheard them talking of Oliver.

Nancy began to cry bitterly

Monks said that Oliver was his younger brother, and he wanted Fagin to arrange to have him killed so that he could get his hands on the boy's fortune.

'I heard Monks mention your name, Miss,' Nancy had explained to Rose, 'and where you were staying in London. That's how I knew where to find you.' Then Nancy began to cry bitterly. 'Please, Miss, don't let darling Oliver come to any harm! I'd give my own life to save him. Honest I would!'

'But what can I do?' Rose had protested. 'How can I find this dreadful Mr Monks?'

'I can help you,' Nancy promised. 'If you'll find a gentleman to help and protect you, I'll tell you where Monks can be found.'

'Where shall we meet you?' asked Rose.

'On London Bridge. I'll be there every Sunday night, between eleven and midnight,' Nancy said.

Mr Brownlow was astonished and intrigued by Rose's story. 'There's a mystery here, right enough,' he said. 'Nancy is taking a great risk for Oliver's sake. She's a very brave soul,' he muttered. 'The thieves and criminals who are her companions will surely kill her if they discover what she has done. Still,' he went on, 'we cannot let this chance slip by. Oliver's fortune, and his life, are at stake. We must meet this girl and learn all we can from her!'

—⟶ ✳ ⟵—

THE MEETING

Nancy was not on London Bridge the first Sunday night, for Bill Sikes, who was in a very bad mood, threatened to beat her if she left the house.

Fagin was there at the time, and he thought there was something very odd about Nancy's manner and behaviour. Why did she so want to go out? He decided to send one of his boys to follow Nancy on the next Sunday night, to see where she went and whom she met.

The spy watched as Nancy met Rose and Mr Brownlow on the bridge just after midnight. Unseen and unheard, the boy crept close and heard Nancy describe the tall, lean Mr Monks, the public house he often visited, and at what times.

'You can recognise him easily,' Nancy said. 'There is a mark on his throat, a big red…'

'A red mark!' Mr Brownlow interrupted her. 'A mark like a burn or a scald?'

'Why, yes!' Nancy replied, surprised. 'Do you know him?'

'Yes, I think I do!' Mr Brownlow muttered nodding grimly.

The very next day, Mr Brownlow went out with two of his menservants to look for Monks. Quite near the public house of which Nancy had spoken, they spotted their prey.

Before Monks knew what was happening, the menservants grabbed him, bundled him into a hackney carriage and drove off to Mr Brownlow's house.

The menservants grabbed him

'Your name is not Monks!'

THE MYSTERY IS SOLVED

Monks was led to a back room.

'Go outside and lock the door!' Mr Brownlow told the menservants. 'Mr Monks and I will speak together alone!'

When the servants had gone, Mr Brownlow looked at Monks sadly for a few moments. *I thought this was the man*, he reflected silently. *Nancy described him well*. Aloud he said, 'Your name is not Monks, it's Edward Leeford!'

Monks gave a start of surprise. 'How d'you know that?' he growled suspiciously.

Mr Brownlow sighed. 'Because I knew your father, Edwin Leeford, and his sister, who died many, many years ago – on the very day she and I were to be married!'

A flicker of pain crossed Mr Brownlow's face as he remembered his young bride-to-be. 'I know that your father and mother were unhappy together, and that they parted when you were still a boy. And…' Mr Brownlow paused for a second. 'I know that you have a brother!'

Monks's eyes narrowed. 'I was an only child!'

'The only child of your father's marriage, yes!' said Mr Brownlow. 'But after your parents parted, your father fell in love with a girl called Agnes Fleming. She died giving birth to their child – a boy who, by the grace of God, later fell into my hands! I knew what Agnes looked like, for your father gave me her portrait, and the boy looked exactly like her!'

———— ✳ ————

Monks was utterly dumbfounded – and the old gentleman hadn't finished. He told how Oliver had disappeared on the way to the bookshop, and how he had searched for him.

'I knew you could solve this mystery for me,' Mr Brownlow told Monks. 'I also knew of your criminal life and that you had escaped to the West Indies. So I followed you!'

The voyage to the West Indies had been fruitless. By the time Mr Brownlow arrived there, Monks had already returned to England. So Mr Brownlow made the long journey home, and once again began searching for Monks. But not until he heard Nancy speak of the man with the scar, did the old gentleman have any clue to where Monks was.

'You were a wretched child, and you are still a scoundrel and a robber!' Mr Brownlow declared. 'You plan to have Oliver murdered, so you can have all your father's money!'

'You can't prove anything!' Monks blustered, turning pale.

'Oh, but I can!' Mr Brownlow retorted. 'I know about Fagin and the plot you hatched together!'

'F-Fagin?' Monks stammered. 'Who is he?'

'Shall we call the police, then, and let you deny it to them?'

Monks looked terrified. 'No, no, don't!' he pleaded. 'They – they will hang me!'

'Then do as I ask!' Mr Brownlow cried. 'Sign a document giving Oliver his rightful share of your father's money!'

Monks looked miserable. He thought of the hangman's rope that would surely be round his neck if he refused.

'Very well,' he muttered. 'Oliver shall have his inheritance.'

— ✳ —

He missed his footing

A BRIGHT FUTURE

Poor Nancy, whose love for Oliver made her take such great risks on his behalf, sadly paid a high price for her actions. When Fagin's spy told him about Nancy's meeting with Rose and Mr Brownlow, Fagin had been enraged. He told Bill Sikes the story. Bill, always a brutal man, took his pistol and cold-heartedly shot Nancy dead.

The very night that Mr Brownlow and Monks had their talk, the police cornered Bill Sikes in his hiding place. In a panic, Bill clambered out onto the roof, taking with him a rope to let himself down to the ground and make his escape. But he missed his footing and as he fell, the rope tangled round his neck. The rope tightened, and Bill choked to death.

That same day, acting on information given to them by Mr Brownlow, the police arrested Fagin, together with several of his boys. Fagin was tried and sent to the gallows.

As for Oliver Twist, Mr Brownlow adopted him as his own son. He took him to live in the country, with Mrs Bedwin. Oliver was very happy there, for he loved the fresh, green countryside, with its beautiful fields and flowers and trees.

Once, Oliver had been a poor, misused orphan boy whose only home was the workhouse. Now, his life was happy and his future was bright. He had the inheritance his father had intended for him. Above all, now that Fagin was dead and his gang broken up, Oliver need never be afraid of them again.

— ✳ —